What Marion Taught Willis

By Brook Berg

Illustrations by Nathan Alberg

Published by UpstartBooks
W5527 Highway 106
P.O. Box 800
Fort Atkinson, Wisconsin 53538-0800
1-800-448-4887

Text © 2005 by Brook Berg
Illustrations © 2005 by Nathan Alberg

The paper used in this publication meets the minimum requirements of American National
Standard for Information Science — Permanence of Paper for Printed Library Material.
ANSI/NISO Z39.48.

To Solomon, who stands at the threshold of all his adventures.
There are so many people to acknowledge and thank: my husband and family who
encourage and support me, the Detroit Lakes Middle School Writers who helped identify
the "stuff" in this story, and the many teacher-librarians
who show students the path to adventure!
—B. B.

To Jim Harris for challenging me, Gary Wolff for teaching me, and my brother Jeremy for
inspiring me. Most of all, to my late Grandpa Alberg, who got me interested in a career
in art when I was just a boy. God bless him.
—N. A.

Everyone in Mr. Owen's class is excited about Career Day. Each student gets to choose a profession, become an expert on it, and then share with the class what he or she learned. No one is more eager than Marion Hedgehog and Willis Anteater.

Shortly before lunch, Mr. Owen announces, "Career Day is coming up next week. When I call your name, I want you to tell the class which career you have chosen to research." As Mr. Owen writes down each student's choice, the class becomes more excited about the assignment.

"Willis, what are you researching?" asks Mr. Owen.

"Firefighting!" Willis exclaims. "My Uncle Dan is a fireman, and he said I could come to the fire hall and interview the whole fire company this weekend!"

"That sounds just great," replies Mr. Owen.

"Marion," asks Mr. Owen, "How about you? What profession are you researching?"

Not to be outdone, Marion proudly proclaims, "Being a librarian. Nothing is more exciting than being a librarian!"

"You've got to be kidding!" laughs Willis. "There is nothing more dull than being in the library with all those old books! What are you going to do, bring in a stack of books and read to us? That will be one boring speech!"

"Willis, that is not the way we talk to each other in this classroom," cuts in Mr. Owen. "It's time to line up for hand washing and lunch. Willis, you will be last in the line."

All through lunch Marion thinks about what Willis said. How could anyone think the library was a boring and dull place? She decides to teach Willis the truth about libraries the very first chance she gets.

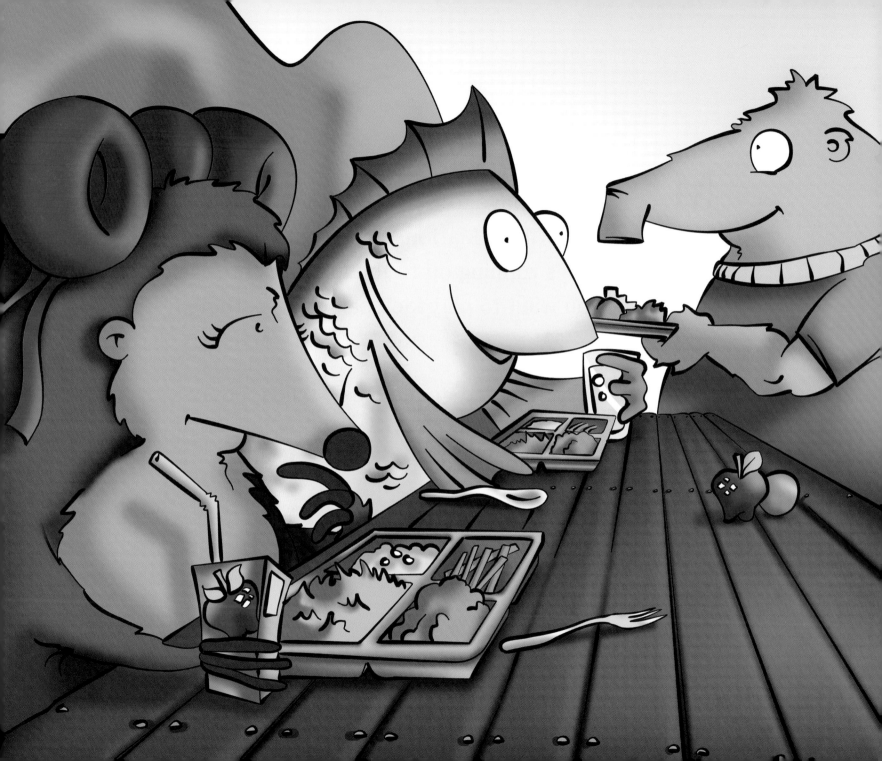

Marion doesn't have to wait long. Right after lunch she sees Willis. "Marion," Willis calls, "You're so weird, always running off to the Media Center. Why don't you want to play kick ball or something fun?"

Marion turns to him and challenges, "Willis, I dare you to come to the Media Center with me and see what I do there! I double dare you!"

"You dare me? Why, you little book-bug," sputters Willis.

"I think you're afraid to come to the Media Center with me because you know that I will prove you wrong," taunts Marion.

"I am not afraid of you or anything in there, I just don't want to waste my recess …"

"Wait till I tell everyone that I dared Willis to come into the Media Center and he wouldn't do it!" Marion interrupts.

"Alright, alright, I'll come," Willis mumbles sourly. "But hurry up. Ernie and I were going to play his Game Boy this afternoon."

As Marion leads Willis to the nonfiction section he says, "Why are we going here? I always get my books there." He points to the picture books. "This side is confusing."

Marion doesn't say anything, just pulls Willis toward a section labeled 200. She picks a book and says, "This book is like the original video game." Marion starts to tell Willis the amazing story—a guy named Perseus *(per-see-us)* went after a Gorgon called Medusa who could turn a person to stone just by looking at him.

As Marion talks, Willis sees Perseus (who looks just like him) swing his great sword to kill Medusa. It is a thrilling story—maybe even better than a video game. Willis wants to read on, but Marion says, "This is just the beginning," and leads him to the 400s.

Marion smiles as she pulls a dictionary from the shelf and says, "Remember last week when I called you 'dynamic' and you got mad? Well, here is what it means—'powerful'—so instead of getting mad, you could have come here and looked it up, then you'd know it was a compliment! Anytime you want to know what a word means or how to say something in a different language just look here!"

"You think I'm powerful?" Willis asks. "Of course," Marion replies as she pulls him along to the 700s.

"You will like this area," Marion announces as she pulls a book with a picture of a guy flying off a half-pipe on the cover.

"Skateboarding!" Willis exclaims. "Wow, I didn't know this was here! Are you telling me that I can find out about anything in this section?" Marion grins and says, "Sure, just try it!"

Willis asks, "Okay, what about fixing my bike?"

Marion replies, "For bikes, go to the 600s because that is where all the mechanical information is found. It's really easy when you know where to look."

"How do you know all this?" Willis wonders.

"I was hoping you'd want to know!" says Marion. She explains, "The man who invented the Dewey system decided that he was going to design a way for all the knowledge ever known in the whole world to be arranged so that anyone looking for anything would be able to find it easily. The Dewey Decimal System is sort of arranged like a person growing up.

"When you're little, a person thinks only of himself. The 100s have all the stuff a person would want to know about himself, like what your dreams or handwriting means, plus things like optical illusions. The 100s are all about you.

"When you get older, you probably start to wonder where everyone came from. Books in the 200s explain the world and the heavens—all the religions and mythologies.

"Once you understand there are other people besides your family in the world and they don't all look or act like you do, you will want to find out more about them. The 300s have all kinds of information about how people live and work. You could find information about firefighters, plus things like holidays and folktales. The 300s are all about the social world.

"You already know the 400s are about language. When you want to talk with the people you learned about in the 300s, that is where you look.

"The 500s are the best! Everything you would ever want to know about science or nature is there. The dinosaur books, the animal books, the books about plants and planets, and science fair projects are in the 500s!

"Eventually, you grow up and have to go to work. The 600s are sometimes called the technology books. I think of them as 'working books' because it's where all the information you learned about in the 500s is used to make or do cool stuff. If you want to know about plants in nature you look in the 500s, but if you want to know how to grow a garden, you look in the 600s. Just like fixing your bike…"

Willis interrupts, "I think I get it now. How wheels work is in the 500s and how to fix my bike is in the 600s."

"Exactly!" Marion replies with a grin.

"When you are done working or have some free time you'll want something fun to do. Go to the 700s, because that is where all of the books about sports, games, hobbies, and music are found."

"Like BMX racing?" asks Willis.

"That's right!" laughs Marion.

"The 800s section is for all the plays, poetry, and other great books people have written. Actually, all the fiction books could be put in the 800s, but since there are so many of them, librarians usually just put them in their own section.

"You'll like the 900s. That's where all the books about countries and famous people and wars are kept. It's also where books about interesting stuff like shipwrecks and people surviving plane crashes are shelved."

"Wow, plane crashes!" blurts Willis. "That sounds outstanding!"

"Finally, Dewey had all this knowledge arranged and thought he was done, but realized that there was a whole category he missed. So he put all of the information like newspapers, encyclopedias, and mysterious things like UFOs and the Bermuda Triangle in the 000s, which, by the way, is pronounced zero hundreds."

"Wow, this really is an amazing place," Willis says. "Even the old books are surprising. I guess the library can be an exciting place when you know where to look. Will you help me find that bike repair book, Marion?"

"We can't now, look at the time, but I can meet you here after school," Marion replies.

"Is recess over already? I was having fun. Okay, I'll be here after school. Race you to class!"

About Brook Berg and Marion the Hedgehog

Brook Berg is the Library Media Specialist in Detroit Lakes, a small town in northern Minnesota. She spends her days at Detroit Lakes Middle School where she teaches students how to find the information and the books they need.

Marion was a real hedgehog who lived with Brook for many years. She often visited the Magelssen Elementary School library where students voted to name her Marion, after Marian the Librarian from *The Music Man.* Marion went to Hedgehog Heaven in 2001.

Brook and Marion liked to read books all year long, walk in Minnesota's north woods during the summer and spend lots of time in the Media Center reading with the students or helping them find good books.

Brook is the author of *What Happened to Marion's Book?* from UpstartBooks.

Marion Hedgehog, the inspiration.